What Could it Be?

EXPLORING THE IMAGINATIVE WORLD OF SHAPES

Sally Fawcett

This shape is a
CIRCLE.

What else could it be?

Can you find a red circle?

Can you find an orange circle?

Can you find a pink circle?

How many other circles can you find?

Corn

Rhubarb

Cabbage

Blue Berries

Carrot

This shape is a
SQUARE.

square

What else could it be?

This is a picture
of Nana and me.

Can you find a yellow square?

Can you find a green square?

Can you find a white square?

How many other squares can you find?

This shape is a
TRIANGLE.

triangle

What else could it be?

This is the mountain
that Dad loves to ski.

Can you find a blue triangle?

Can you find a **black** triangle?

Can you find a purple triangle?

How many other triangles can you find?

This shape is a
RECTANGLE.

rectangle

What else could it be?

This is my treasure chest
locked with a key.

Can you find a brown rectangle?

Can you find a red rectangle?

Can you find a white rectangle?

How many other rectangles can you find?

This shape is a
HEXAGON.

hexagon

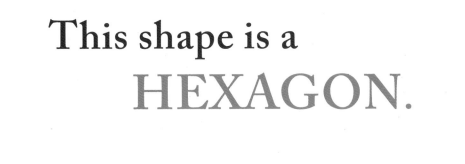

What else could it be?

This is a spider's
web hung in a tree.

Can you find a grey hexagon?

Can you find a yellow hexagon?

Can you find a pink hexagon?

How many other hexagons can you find?

This shape is an
OVAL.

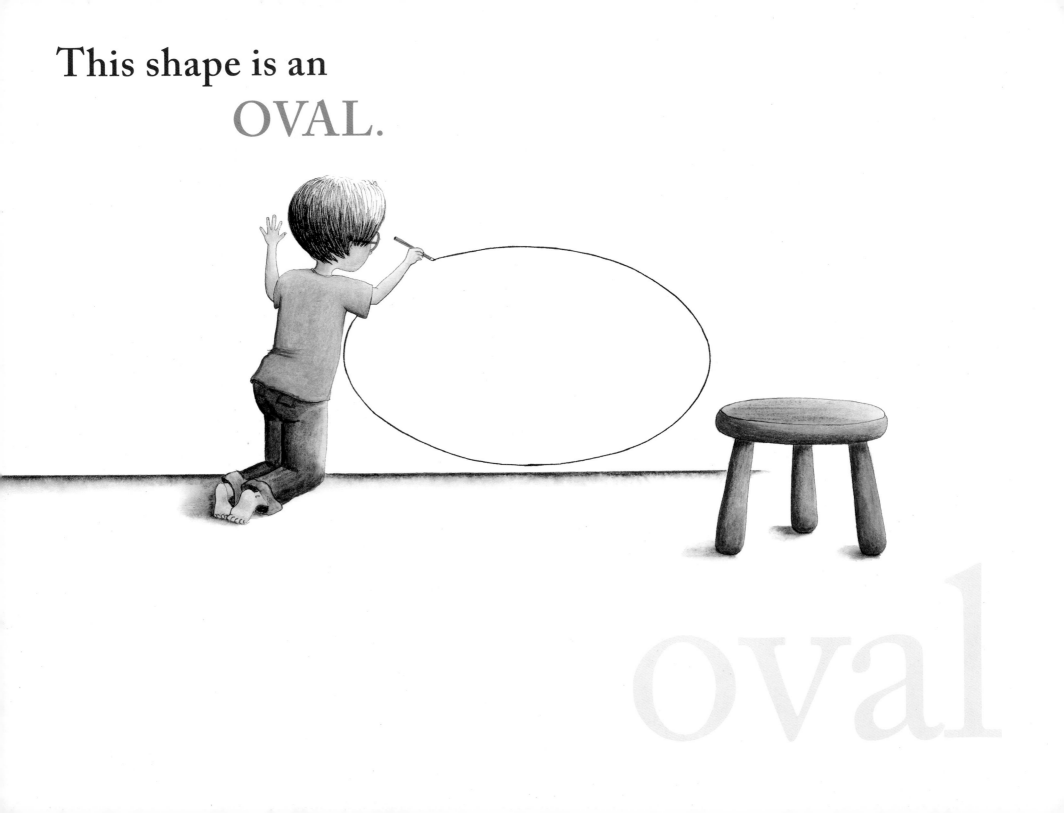

oval

What else could it be?

This is the pot for our afternoon tea.

Can you find a blue oval?

Can you find an orange oval?

Can you find a green oval?

How many other ovals can you find?

octagon

This shape is an
OCTAGON.

What else could it be?

This is a parasol
down by the sea.

Can you find a **black** octagon?

Can you find a purple octagon?

Can you find a brown octagon?

How many other octagons can you find?

So now that your thinking is out of the square,

pull out a pencil and pull up a chair.

If you are willing, and if you so choose,

here are some ways to make templates to use.

DOWNLOAD: Downloadable templates are available
at www.whatcoulditbe.ekbooks.com.au

TRACE: Lay a sheet of paper over the shape pages
and trace over the shape to get you started.

CREATE: Make your own template, using a computer, by
selecting a shape of your choice and printing out a page to draw on.

Then if you would like to, and if you agree,
I'd love you to share your ideas with me!

UPLOAD: Visit www.whatcoulditbe.ekbooks.com.au
to find out how you can upload your artwork for others to see.

First published 2016

EK Books

an imprint of Exisle Publishing Pty Ltd

'Moonrising', Narone Creek Road, Wollombi, NSW 2325, Australia

P.O. Box 60–490, Titirangi, Auckland 0642, New Zealand

www.ekbooks.com.au

Copyright © 2016 in text and illustrations: Sally Fawcett

Sally Fawcett asserts the moral right to be identified as the creator of this work.

A CiP record for this book is available from the National Library of Australia.

ISBN 978-1-925335-02-6

Designed by Big Cat Design

Typeset in Adobe Caslon Pro 18 on 20pt

Printed in China

This book uses paper sourced under ISO 14001 guidelines from well-managed forests and other controlled sources.

10 9 8 7 6 5 4 3 2 1